ZONDERKIDZ

7 Days of Awesome
Copyright © 2016 by Shawn Byous
Illustrations © 2016 by Colin Jack

This title is also available as a Zondervan ebook.
Visit www.zondervan.com/ebooks

Requests for information should be addressed to:

Zonderkidz, 3900 Sparks Dr. SE, Grand Rapids, Michigan 49546

ISBN 978-0-310-74349-1

Design: Kris Nelson

Printed in China

15 16 17 18 19 20 21 22 23 24 25 /DHC/ 16 15 14 13 12 11 10 9 8 7 6 5 4 3 2 1

7 DAYS OF AWESOME

By Shawn Byous
Illustrated by Colin Jack

ZONDERkidz

Have you thought of these things?
Well, maybe you should.
So wake up your mind!
It will do you some good!

Where did fish come from?
Or even these rocks?

GOD WAS THERE AND HE HAD A PLAN. AND THIS IS HOW IT ALL BEGAN...

It's OUTTA SIGHT!!

God first made the light.

And why would that be?

'Cause there's so much to see!

God called it all good.
That's the end of Day 1.

Day 2 is HUGE!

And do you know why?
On day number two,
God made the big sky!

With water above,
and water below,

God made the sky high,

and He made the ground low.

See all the seas?
And see all the trees?
On Day number 3,
God made all of these!

And LOOK! What a hoot!
Today, God made fruit!

Isn't that neat?
Now there's something to eat!

Then God said with glee,
"It looks good to Me!"

So that, my dear friend,
is the end of Day 3!

Then on Day 4
God made even more!

The moon and the stars—
outer space to explore!

God filled up the skies
with treats for our eyes!
The highest of heights
is now full of lights!

Things are ALIVE on Day number 5!

With just a few words,
God made all the birds!

And not only birds,
but in the same way ...
He made all the fish,
on that very same day!

God filled up the seas,
and He filled up the sky,
with fish that could swim,
and birds that could fly!

And not only you,
the entire ZOO TOO!

Some that are short, and some that are TALL!

God made EYES
for seeing ...

God made HAIR
for growing ...

God made us to love, and He made us to live.

He made arms to hug,

and He made hands to give.

Yes, God made it all,
like no one else could.
All to glorify Him,
and He called it all good!

On Day 7 God made
what I like BEST!

Do YOU know what He made ...?

That's when God made **REST!**